MURDER AT TURTLE CREEK

By
Loretta Toussant

Copyright © 2020 by Loretta Toussant

All rights reserved. No part of this book may be used or reproduced by any means, graphic, electronic, or mechanical, including photocopying, recording, taping, or by any information storage retrieval system, without the written permission of the publisher except in the case of brief quotations embodied in critical articles and reviews.

Dedication

This is dedicated to the memory of the late "Mary Ann Perry - Jennings" who suggested that I write a book.

TABLE OF CONTENTS

CHAPTER 1 1

CHAPTER 2 7

CHAPTER 3 9

CHAPTER 4 11

CHAPTER 5 17

CHAPTER 6 21

CHAPTER 7 27

CHAPTER 8 29

C HAP TE R 9 33

CHAPTER 1

The days are getting longer in late March. The trees are starting to sprout, and the water is rising in Turtle Creek. Brothers Casey and Caleb Jones are out scrounging the bayou after school before their Dad Peter calls them in for supper.

"I'm gonna find a 50-pound snapping turtle," a determined Casey tells Caleb. The day is mild while the moist clay pungent smell of the bayou is apparent as the boys scour the banks searching for treasure. A menacing black buzzard glistening from moisture from the Louisiana foliage glistening, dives towards something at the bayous' darkness, the brothers turn towards the commotion, they then notice something floating near the surface of the murky shallow water. They creep towards what seems to be occupying the birds' attention, what looks like a blue hued fabric seems to float near the surface, as they move closer, they see that the blue hued fabric is covering what seems to be a human body! The terrified boys start running towards town to the Town of Rice Police Station. Once there they encounter St Luke's sheriff deputy, Stanford Rideau who attempts to slow the boys down for better understanding, " Hold up slow down" as the excited young boys try to describe what they've seen! " "Ok Ok he says in a doubtful voice, I'll send somebody down there," Deputy Rideau picks up his radio and begrudgingly dispatches a fellow deputy to the bayou. After being told to "Get along Home" the boys stand and watch as a police cruiser moves towards the water. Deputy Tim Douglas being first on scene, examines the area around the bayou then proceeds towards the area where the boys spotted the suspicious sighting. Tim goes to the trunk and pulls out a pair of waders then moves down the bayou bank. "Oh my God," he utters as he gets closer to what is obviously a floating body! Tim then radios back to headquarters his recent discovery.

Her long tanned legs entwined with his; the soft swell of her breast snuggled against his chest was the makings of a perfect spring afternoon. Detective Blaine Bienvenuee was blissfully content in the embrace of his longtime girlfriend, Leigh. Today was her off day from waitressing at Fat Daddy's Bar and Grill. For him an afternoon exploring the silky warmth of her body always allowed him to escape the cold starkness of enforcing the law. His cell phone began its familiar dance on the nightstand summoning him back to his reality. " Bienvenue" he growled as he responded to the male voice on the other end of the phone.

The black Indian Scout Vintage styled motorcycle with the suede camel colored fringes adorning its saddle bags danced delicately in the mild breeze revealing that lieutenant Maria Duplessis was present and accounted for. Her tall always fit yet generously curvy body clothed in her usual snug fitting jeans tee shirt and cowboy boots, her long naturally curly hair flows over her shoulders the top tied back with a simple red bandana was crouched over the floating object which had been confirmed as the remains of a female body.

As Blaine Approached the scene Maria says, "Well it's about time you make an appearance Mr. Bienvenue!" "What do we have here?" says Blaine, "A Black female approximately 17 years old. Looking at the condition of the body I'd say she's been in the water about 12hrs or more. Jose is on the way from a conference in Lafayette he'll give us a true time of death. The clothes seem to be a school uniform from Sacred Heart of Jesus private school. We'll have to check with the school office to see who's been absent that meets her description to try an identify her." "So how did she die"? Blaine asked. "Her throat was cut, she probably bled out before she was left here," says Bienvenue.

Maria, after retiring as an Army MP Sergeant, returned to St Luke's Parish to care for her aging father. Her mother passed away a couple of years before. After her return she joined the St Luke's

Sheriffs' office and quickly moved up to lenient due to her military experience and her natural instincts.

Blaine was 3rd generation law enforcement in St Luke's Parish, his Father Blaine Bienvenue Sr. was a retired detective, his grandfather, Benjamin Bienvenue serves as sheriff from 1964- 1999 so he had big shoes to fill. Blaine left St Luke's parish to work in Orleans Parish. He really enjoyed the faster pace Orleans offered, but eventually drifted back toward his roots. His Cajun rugged, yet handsome looks were both a gift and a curse. The daily five mile runs kept him in tip top shape even with his weakness for Leigh's rich Creole cooking, the naturally tanned skin thick and his close cropped wavy hair was a true testament of his Cajun and French heritage.

" Let's rope off the east and West banks of the bayou and scope out the area for footprints, Also let's check the rails of turtle creek bridge for fingerprints, just in case the body was thrown from there," says Blaine, "Good possibility that she was killed elsewhere then dumped here. With all the stumps in the water it isn't likely she floated far!"

After the body was retrieved from the water and bagged, the officers present took a closer look at the dead girl. "Oh, sweet Jesus! That looks like Ms. Peg Quincy's granddaughter, Liz!" Says Tim Douglas, she's the spitting image of her Mama Jessie Mae! This is going to kill poor Ms. Peg!" While zipping the body into the bag, a laminated school ID dangling from the victims' neck was caught in the zipper. Maria stepped forward taking the plastic badge into her still gloved hand read the name typed beneath the plastic coating, "Elizabeth Quincy, Sacred Heart of Jesus High School."

After the body was transported to the parish morgue, the officers on the scene convened in Sheriff Shane Doggon's office along with District Attorney, Sam Cashio. "Well folks, looks like we got ourselves a murder, says Shane and being that it seems to be a 17-year-old girl it isn't gonna be nothing nice in this town! Tim, being that you know the family, I'm going to ask you to notify them and have someone come to the morgue and identify the body." A mixture sorrow and regret showed on Tim's face as he responded, "Yes sir, I'll head on out there soon as we're through here."

CHAPTER 2

The day after the body was identified, Coroner Jose Gutierrez determined that girl had indeed died from a severed carotid artery. She seemed to have been a healthy 17- year-old girl before her untimely death. To his surprise she was three months pregnant! Scrapings were taken from beneath her fingernails and preserved for DNA testing as well as tissue samples from the fetus. The body was checked for defensive wounds or scrapes, none were found.

Maria was assigned to question students and faculty of Sacred Heart of Jesus High School. Grief counselors were on hand at the small campus to offer comfort and answer any questions as to how this could have happened to this seemingly beloved student. After interviewing several students along with the principal and Sister Margaret, it appeared that Liz had been a very bright and outgoing student. She was on the honor roll every school year and captain of the varsity volleyball team her junior and senior year. Due to the pregnancy Maria asked the students if they knew of Liz having a boyfriend. Coco Dotson, a petite light skinned black girl was said to be Liz's best friend, visibly shaken by the loss, with tears rolling streaming down her freckled cheeks, Coco only managed to shake her head no, with her long auburn braids twirling across her small shoulders. Maria pulled the girl into an embrace in effort to comfort her sorrow. Maria gave the girl her card and asked her to call if she remembers anything.

CHAPTER 3

He ran his right pointer finger across the blade of the hunting knife. It had been given to him by his father when he was a young boy, the leather wrapping on the handle was worn and fraying but the blade was still razor- sharp do to regular sharpening on his trusty stone worn smooth from years of use. He'd used the knife to dress countless hunted deer. He'd also used it to remove the testicles of male calves of the cattle he raised. He'd never used it on a human until he had to kill the girl! She gave him no choice! She wanted to keep the baby! He'd offered her money for an abortion, but she refused due to her Catholic beliefs. She wouldn't kill her child.

He offered her a ride from school and after she was out of eye sight of the school, he stopped pretending something was wrong with the tire. After he'd gotten out of the vehicle, she followed to see what was going on. He then grabbed her long silky hand in his fist pulling the sharp blade across her delicate mocha colored throat. Her eyes bulged and her mouth opened and closed making low gurgling sounds as the life quickly left her body. Blood poured down the front of the light blue uniform shirt pooling at her feet. He'd carefully been sure to keep the girl in front of him avoiding spurts of blood from the dying body. He dragged the body several feet onto the wooden bridge and threw her over the metal hand rail while being careful not to leave finger prints. He had thought to bring a bag of lime and used it to cover the blood trail using his boot to blend it with the dust and gravel of the road. Being that this area of town was seldom traveled he had the time to cover his tracks without being seen.

CHAPTER 4

A week after the autopsy was completed, the body was released to the family for burial.

Due to the decomposed state of the body the family made the agonizing decision to cremate the remains. The coroner, Dr. Gutierrez concluded that the body had been in the water for at least 12 hours. The wildlife of the bayou had wreaked havoc on it.

A week after the memorial service, Blaine and Maria paid a visit to Liz family for questioning. The DNA evidence from beneath her fingernails and from her unborn child hadn't matched anyone in the nationwide data base so it was time to formally launch the investigation of this truly heinous crime. Her grandmother was sitting on the porch fanning with a church fan, even though it was a cool Louisiana morning. Wearing a worn Grey wool sweater casually around her shoulders and her long Grey hair pinned into a simple French twist and small pearl earrings adding a touch of elegance to the lined caramel skin, her eyes were moist and swollen from the constant flow of tears.

"Hey Ms. Peg," said Maria, I think you know Blaine my coworker. "So sorry for your lost Ma'am," said Blaine. Thank you, baby, I knew ya Daddy and I taught your older brother at the high school. "Ms. Peg did you know Liz was pregnant? Asked Maria, "No, I did not! My Lizzy wasn't fast like that! " she went to school, got good grades, said she'd like to be a doctor someday, Ms. Peg said." "Did she have a boyfriend," asked Blaine?" "I've raised Liz since her Mama died when she was 10 and she could talk to me about anything, I think she would have told me if she was serious with anybody, of course as pretty as she was, boys were sniffing around but she didn't pay them no mind, said she wanted a career first," said Ms. Peg. "that night she didn't come home I called the police right away because she wasn't one to run the streets all night. They told me she was probably hanging out with friends, but I knew in my gut something was wrong!" "Did she ever have trouble with anybody," asked Blaine? "No sir," she said. "Everybody loved Lizzy she was a sweet child and not just because she was mine! Everybody will tell you the same thing!"

"Well thank you for your time Ms. Peg and we promise to do everything we can to find out who did this," said Maria. "Blaine nodded in agreement. "Ms. Maria I know your people as well and I believe you'll do your best to find out who took that baby's life," said Ms. Peg.

As they drove off in their unmarked unit, Blaine said, "I could really use a cup of coffee, a shot of Makers Mark would be better if I wasn't working, ok if stop over at Fat Daddy's?" "Fine with me," said Maria.

Leigh was wiping down the long-polished wood counter. The building had been there since the 1940's, the current owner had remodeled it but kept its original feel. "Hey y'all," she said!

"Y'all look like two whooped puppy dogs (need name for owner of bar)!" "We just left Ms. Peg's house, said Blaine. "That poor woman, bless her heart, buried her only daughter now her granddaughter, Lawd have mercy," Leigh said, shaking her head, her shiny black curls bouncing as she spoke.

"Gotta tell y'all something too, heard some talk that Ray-Ray Rile had been known to follow Liz around." Ray Ray," or "Crazy Ray Ray," as he was best known around town. He was called that because he received a government disability check or a crazy check due to not being quite right in the head. He didn't drive so he delivered groceries to old people on a rusty old bike with a basket on the front.

"As far as I know Ray-Ray has always been pretty harmless, just likes to chat up the ladies," says Maria. He's even hemmed me up now and then she laughed." "Well I hear he got a little more intense with Liz, I hear he showed up at her house

13

one day with flowers and a bubble gum ring, got down on one knee and told her she could be his wife if she wanted to," says Leigh, her golden cat light eyes widening with excitement as she spoke! "Bless his heart," says Blaine. "He seems harmless but we'll check it out, thanks for the info darlin," mindlessly running his hand over his close cropped wavy hair.

Ray-Ray lived in a small rundown travel trailer on the other side of the track, his Mama died when he was young, so relatives and other folks in town always looked out for him. He was now in his 50's but had the mind of a child. They found him sitting in the yard in an old bucket seat from a car, beneath the small porch cover that he had haphazardly built over the side entrance to the trailer. As Blaine and Maria walked into the yard, he shouts "What y'all want, I ain't did nothing and I don't like no Po Po! So just git on way from here!" "Hey Hey, calm down Ray Ray we just want to talk," says Blaine. "I don't wanna talk to you! Cause you the Po Po and a hard leg, I'll talk to huh tho," he said while breaking into a big grin. "She some pretty," said Ray-Ray. Blaine looked over at Maria with a smirk. "Well hey there Ray Ray," says Maria, "How you doin? " I'm better now that you Here brutiful!" "That's nice she says; can I ask you some questions please?" "Ok, he says, his crossed eyes staring blankly at her. "I wanna ask you about Liz Quincy?" "Huh dead he said with a sad expression on his worn leather like chocolate skin, the now grey hair sparsely covering his scalp looked like cotton stuffing from an old chair, huge tears pooled in his rusty colored eyes as he spoke. "Did you kill her," asked Maria pointedly? " I ain't kilted huh! I love did huh!" "Well maybe you got mad because she wouldn't marry you and killed her," says Blaine. I dun killed birds and squirrels with my be be gun, I ain't killed no people! They ghost might come back and git me," he says shaking his head looking suddenly frightened! " Ok Ray Ray, says Maria we're gonna go now and leave you be, but if you hear somethin you come tell me ok?" "Yes, Ma'am I will, I hope y'all git who killed my Liz, she was gonna be my wife," he says, the childlike cadence returning to his voice.

CHAPTER 5

After bringing Sheriff Doggone up to date on the investigation, Shane and Maria called it a day, Blaine headed back to Fat Daddy's and Maria headed home to her humble abode. Her home had been in her family for years, having once been a share cropper's shack, bought from a sugar cane farmer then moved to its present spot further down the bayou from where the body had been found. A shiver ran down Maria's spine at the thought of the young girl being found in the peaceful bayou that meandered thru the sleepy town and ended at Maria's quiet spot away from everything.

The little cypress home had been updated many times over the years. After the passing of her Father, Maria added an all-weather porch to the rear of the house, designed with both modern glass walls and screened windows that could open to allow the fresh country air to flow through. Often times the sweet smell of sugar cane wafted through the room this time of the year and a chorus of chirping crickets was a welcomed soundtrack to the end of the day.

Her two companions, Jazzy, her black and white fur ball Shih Tzu and her loyal Golden Retriever Zeus greeted her at the door with tails wagging.

Maria had ended a seven- year relationship with the man she still considered her soul mate and best friend. They enjoyed many great times over the years. He was the one she could talk to about anything. His even tempered and happy go lucky nature was always a welcome change to the day to day challenges of the job.

They met when he evacuated from New Orleans during Hurricane Katrina. He was her cousin's best friend since high school and had readily accepted his invitation to ride out the storm in Rice. They hit it off immediately after being introduced. That normally never happened with Maria, being in law enforcement made her a natural cynic, always looking for an agenda, but somehow Jean Lee St Amant was able to break through the armored barriers that she had placed around her heart after two messy divorces. The undivided attention he paid her and the respect he showed for her detailed investigative skill, he was truly the muse that she'd never had before or since.

They enjoyed many thrill seeking adventures together, from riding their motorcycles to the bike rally in Sturgess to weekend canoe rides in the lakes of local state parks.

The love-making was also immensely satisfying from the very first time. At 51 he was as physically fit as he had been when he played wide receiver at LSU in the 70s. The close-cropped silver hair with a matching well-groomed beard against the deep dark chocolate skin topped off the total package of the handsome yet humble man.

Everything was near perfect until she began to question where the relationship was headed. He was very honest in saying he loved her dearly but wasn't ready to settle down into domestic bliss. After seven years she couldn't see a purpose in investing more time, although the most satisfying relationship of her life it

wasn't going anywhere.

One Sunday afternoon after discussing the future of their union she told him that it was time that they called it quits, feeling as though if he truly loved her as he said he did he'd readily propose telling the world that she was his alone. He simply picked up his worn leather duffle bag threw it into the front seat of his old Jeep Wrangler, wearing a sad defeated look, climbed in and drove away down tree lined bayou road. Maria stood there watching him drive away, with tears streaming down her cheeks wanting to stop him yet knowing this is what she had to do for her peace of mind and self-preservation.

CHAPTER 6

The next morning Shane and Maria were summoned back to Sheriff Doggon's office. When they arrived Assistant DA Rosalind Cummings was seated in one of the high-backed leather chairs facing the Sheriffs Massive Antique desk. "ADA Cummings, has some information on the Quincy murder, " he says. Maria's thick dark brows shot up at this statement, Blaine's hands rested at both sides of his waist beneath his shoulder gun holster. Rosalind dressed in a stylish knee length pencil skirt and stylish side bow colored red blouse stood took a deep breath and spoke. "I've been informed that you interviewed my daughter, CoCo Dotson?" Shane and Maria looked at each each other then back to Rosalind. "Dotson is my maiden name," she stated. "Well anyway, no worries, you followed proper legal procedure by questioning with permission from an adult at the school, "Coco has not been herself lately. She's not sleeping nor eating properly, I got her into private counseling and she then admitted that she knew more about Liz's personal life than she'd previously disclosed," She said. "Well that's interesting," says Maria, so Liz was involved with someone?" "She was", says Rosalind, I'd like to bring her in, and you can take her complete statement, I want her to always take full responsibility for both her words and actions. School is being dismissed early on Thursday, so I can have her here for 2pm if that works for you. My only court case that day is at 8am so that should give me plenty of time to get her here," she says in her clear but rapid-fire way of speaking, her Amber colored eyes flashing as she spoke. She then stood. The reddish-brown bob hair style brushing her shoulders as she moved flattering the cappuccino colored skin. Picking up the designer briefcase, she left saying "We'll see you all on Thursday."

Coco's statement did indeed reveal the name and whereabouts of Liz's previously unknown suitor and possibly the father of her unborn child. According to what she said the man in question was handsome, blond-haired blue eyed, Brandon Forte. His father owned the largest cattle ranches in the parish, located in a neighboring town. It seemed that Liz had met him at a party the summer before and they kept their relationship a secret not knowing if their families would accept the interracial Union, after all this was still rural south Louisiana.

Brandon was a freshman at ULL Lafayette and they would secretly meet whenever he was home for the weekend, the campus being 45 miles away from Rice. The couple planned to disclose their relationship that spring after Liz's graduation and 18th birthday.

After this revelation, it was decided to call Brandon into the Sheriff's office for questioning. That Friday afternoon after his last class, he pulled into the police station in his late model Navy Blue Ford F-150 Platinum edition pickup truck, sending dust and gravel flying as he parked. Shane was standing near the front desk as he walked through the front doors, the stride of his '6'ft2" muscular frame alluded confidence but was overshadowed by obvious grief in the sky-blue eyes. "Why am I here," he asked? "I already told you I knew Liz but hadn't seen her in a while." "Mr. Forte can you step into our office please, so that we can have some privacy," Blaine asked? Brandon nodded and followed him down the hallway. Maria was already seated at a desk and asked him to have a seat, "Can get you something to drink?" she added. "Can I get a bottle of water I came straight from school," He asked. She reached into the office mini fridge and handed one to him. He took a long swig finishing it in two gulps. "Wow you were thirsty," says Maria, while taking the empty bottle and carefully placing it into the wastebasket beneath the desk. "I guess I was, thank you Ma'am," he said. They were then interrupted by the buzz of the phone's intercom. "Scuse me y'all but Mr Forte's daddy is here along with his Lawyer, Mr Cashio," says the desk Sargent. Blaine gave Maria a look that said, "I'm not surprised," then said with a sigh, "Bring em in." The door to the office opens and in barrels Joe Cashio while saying "Don't say another word Brandon," following him into the office was Brandon's father, Landon Forte wearing an aggravated scowl across his rugged features, the still thick but greying hair hung over the sun tortured brow, thick callused hands rested at the waist band of the worn wrangler jeans he wore, a bowie knife with a leather wrapped handle sheathed in a leather holder hung from a heavy western belt.

"Let's go Brandon," said Cashio, sweat beading on his broad forehead, the dark hair damp with perspiration, the Hickie Freeman suit he wore strained to cover his Italian bulk. He was leaving court after a lengthy trial day when he got the call from Forte, demanding that he meet him at the police station, his son had gone there against his advice.

When Landon Forte called, you answered! He had been retained as his personal Attorney for over twenty years and his Father had been the Attorney for the Forte family before him. The business relationship between the families went back over fifty years.

Landon Forte was a third generation Cattleman. His 400 plus herd of Black Angus Cattle was known to be the best beef cattle in the state and always brought top dollar due to being bred from only the best bloodlines. Brandon was expected to carry on the family legacy.

Cashio had huffed and puffed his way from the

nearby courthouse, and was trying not to show how out of breath he was.

As Brandon stood to leave, Blaine nodded towards Cashio while saying to him, "you'll be hearing from me us soon". As Blaine and Maria followed them out of the room, they noticed Landon glaring angrily at his son as the door to the station closed noisily behind them.

"We'll all right then", says Maria, from behind her back she pulled the water bottle that Brandon had drank from, carefully wrapped in a paper towel, wearing a mischievous grin she said, " I guess we better get this to the lab asap for D n a testing. "Good girl", says Blaine.

The following Tuesday morning the DNA evidence from the water bottle had been identified, and the results compared to Liz's fetus, and the scrapings from beneath her nails. The results showed that there was a 99.9% possibility that Brandon Fort'e was indeed the father of her child! The scrapings from beneath her nails also matched, which also meant that they may have also found her killer!

CHAPTER 7

"Something just doesn't smell right to me about this case", says Maria. "All of the evidence points to Brandon, but I don't get a killers vibe from him." Does Brandon have any brothers?", asked Blaine, frowning as he spoke. "As far as I know he's an only child, his mother died when he was young, his Daddy raised him on his own," answered Maria.

"Wait just a god damned minute," says Blaine while jumping to his feet. "A father and son would have nearly identical DNA and if Landon knew that Brandon had gotten Liz pregnant, I don't think he'd be really happy about it! "Did you happen to notice that Bowie knife strapped to Landon's belt when he was here," asked Maria, her golden-brown eyes flashing fire. They both nodded to each other in agreement. "Could sure as hell be the murder weapon." "Well I'll be a monkey's uncle," says Blaine, let's get a judge to subpoena cell phone records from both Landon and Brandon."

CHAPTER 8

The cell phone records showed that Brandon called Liz's cell phone at 7:30 on the night that she was killed. His phone records showed that he had indeed pinged a cell tower in Lafayette near the university! Landon's phone on the other hand pinged a cell tower in Rice, very close to where Liz's body was dumped!

After updating sheriff Doggone, Then presenting probable cause to a judge, an arrest warrant was issued for none other than Landon Forte.

With the warrant in hand, it was decided that Maria, Blaine, the Sheriff and two other deputies would confront Landon at the ranch. The would proceed cautiously, due to it being a known fact that Landon kept a large collection of weapons, some dating back to the Civil war era.

"This might get ugly, so I'll take my bike up the

logging trail in the back of the property, My Daddy used to break horses for the Forte's when I was a kid so I know a short cut", says Maria.

The smell of the large oak trees that canopied the long graveled driveway to the hundred plus year old ranch house was in the air. The stately old home loomed bright white up ahead, the wrap around gallery style porch which had hosted many parties in its heyday sat empty except for the four large cypress rocking chairs that adorned pine floors which still shinned brightly from many coats of slick varnish.

Years before, the Forte's had been known for their lavish yet down home barbecues which hosted hundreds. Landon didn't inherit the need to socialize from his forefathers, he chose to focus on the running of the ranch only, especially after losing Brandon's mother to cancer, other than business associates he had few friends or guest. He simply didn't see the point

The high-tech cameras mounted almond the driveway alerted Landon to their approach. As the police units neared the house Landon walked out on the porch carrying a Winchester 30/30 rifle, the weapon was powerful enough to cut a man in half! Blaine, the Sheriff and the deputies unholstered their weapons." Put the rifle down", says the Sheriff into bullhorn. "Why are y'all on my property," shouts back Landon. The Bowie knife hung in its usual place on the tooled brown leather belt on his side. "We have a warrant for your arrest, for the murder of Elizabeth Quincy," says the Sheriff, put down your weapon now!"" I'm telling you now, I ain't goin to jail for killing that little nigger gal! Ain't no way she was bringing me no half nigger grandchild!" " I told Brandon to make her get rid of it, but he wouldn't, so I had to take matters into my own hands."

Maria parked the Indian off the trail and quietly made her through the back pasture and onto left side of the gallery. She always had her western styled boots soled in rubber to keep her steps as quiet as possible, from the shoulder holster worn beneath the worn leather motorcycle jacket, she pulled out glock 40 caliber equipped with a laser sight. She had been an expert with both handguns and m16s as an Army mp.

Landon raised the rifle while saying "I'll kill everyone of y'all before I let you take me to jail for this bullshit, I was protecting my family! If that little nigger gal thought she was gonna get her hands on all of this, it wouldn't gonna happen!" Just as he was raising the rifle to aim, Maria fired, the 40-caliber hollow point bullet piercing straight through Landon's right hand, he screamed, "Goddamn you!" as he dropped the rifle. Blaine rushed onto the porch kicking the rifle away and handcuffing Brandon's hands behind him, a steady stream of blood dripped from the handcuffs onto the shiny porch floor. The ceiling fans whirled above them as Landon lay face down on the porch floor.

A cloud of dust rose as Brandon drove up the

driveway, stopping abruptly after seeing all of the commotion. When he sees his father lying on the porch with blood dripping from his hand, he screams, "What have y'all done to my Daddy?" "Brandon, we came here to arrest him, and he aimed his rifle threatening to kill us, an ambulance is on the way he'll be fine" says Maria. "Arrest him for what?" says Brandon. " Murder," says Blaine. "We had enough evidence for a warrant, then he just admitted to killing Liz. "Oh My God Daddy no!" says Landon, how could you do that, I loved Liz! I was going to marry her when she graduated!" "Over my dead body you would marry that nigger"! Visibly shaken, with tears streaking his handsome face, Brandon says to his father, "You are dead to me!" and walks away.

CHAPTER 9

The hundreds of high quality Black Angus cattle lazily grazed in the pastures surrounding the sprawling ranch oblivious to the uncertainty of their future as the ambulance carrying Landon Forte drove away with sirens blaring.

After filling out all of the necessary paper work and giving their account of what happened to the DA, Blaine and Maria headed to the Red Cat for a much needed cold beer. "That was some mighty good shootin," Blaine says to Maria. "Probably saved my hide," he laughed. "All in a day's work partner," she says with a grin. "I'm just glad we can give closure to Liz's family and friends." "I'll drink to that" says Blaine raising his beer mug.

Special Thanks

Special Thanks Special Thank you to "Patrick Fabre" and Carl Toussant Sr. for their expertise in weaponry and police procedure. I would also like to thank my parents Albert Toussant III and Lucille Perry Toussant for reading to me and telling me bedtime stories as a child, it totally sparked my love for books and stories!

Made in the USA
Coppell, TX
16 August 2023